Elmer Blunt's Open House

by Matt Novak

ORCHARD BOOKS • NEW YORK

Copyright © 1992 by Matt Novak
First Orchard Paperbacks edition 1996

ORCHARD BOOKS
95 Madison Avenue
New York, NY 10016

Manufactured in the United States of America
Printed by Barton Press, Inc.
Bound by Horowitz/Rae
Book design by Alice Lee Groton
The text of this book is set in 21.5 pt. ITC Korinna.
The illustrations are watercolor and colored pencil,
reproduced in full color.

Hardcover   10   9   8   7   6   5   4   3   2
Paperback   10   9   8   7   6   5   4   3   2   1

Library of Congress Cataloging-in-Publication Data

Novak, Matt.
    Elmer Blunt's open house / by Matt Novak.
        p.   cm.
    Summary: Several animals and a robber explore
Elmer Blunt's home when he forgets to close the door
on his way to work.
    ISBN 0-531-05998-7 (tr.)
    ISBN 0-531-08598-8 (lib. bdg.)
    ISBN 0-531-07074-3 (pbk.)
    [1. Dwellings—Fiction.   2. Animals—Fiction.
3. Robbers and outlaws—Fiction.]   I. Title.
PZ7.N867E1   1992   [E]—dc20   91-38424

Reprinted by arrangement with Orchard Books.

To Victoria

One morning Elmer Blunt overslept.

He was late for work

and did not close the door properly.

Some animals saw the open door

and went into the house.

They explored the kitchen,

the living room,

the bathroom,

and the bedroom.

They heard a noise downstairs

and hid in the closet.

Someone else had discovered the open door.

The thief explored Elmer Blunt's house.

"Furs!" he exclaimed.

"They're ALIVE!" he howled.

He ran down the stairs,

through the house,

and out the door,

slamming it behind him.

That night when Elmer Blunt came home from work,

he said, "I really made a mess this morning!"

So he cleaned every room,

and he went to sleep

in his safe, quiet home.